THE
Leaky
Story

JJ
SILLETT
DEVON

For Jay, Aaron and Matt, who fill my pen with ink. To Mom and Dad, who gave it to me in the first place. — D.S.

For Deniz and Ada. — A.T.

First published 2017

EK Books
an imprint of Exisle Publishing Pty Ltd
'Moonrising', Narone Creek Road, Wollombi, NSW 2325, Australia
P.O. Box 60–490, Titirangi, Auckland 0642, New Zealand
www.ekbooks.org

A CiP record for this book is available from the National Library of Australia.

ISBN 978-1-925335-39-2

Designed by Big Cat Design
Typeset in Kentuckyfried 19 on 27pt
Printed in China

This book uses paper sourced under ISO 14001 guidelines from well-managed forests and other controlled sources.

10 9 8 7 6 5 4 3 2 1

THE Leaky Story

A fun-filled adventure into the power of the imagination and the magic of books!

Devon Sillett & Anil Tortop

EK

The book sat.

And sat.

And sat.

The black letters were bursting to be
read by someone with a big imagination.

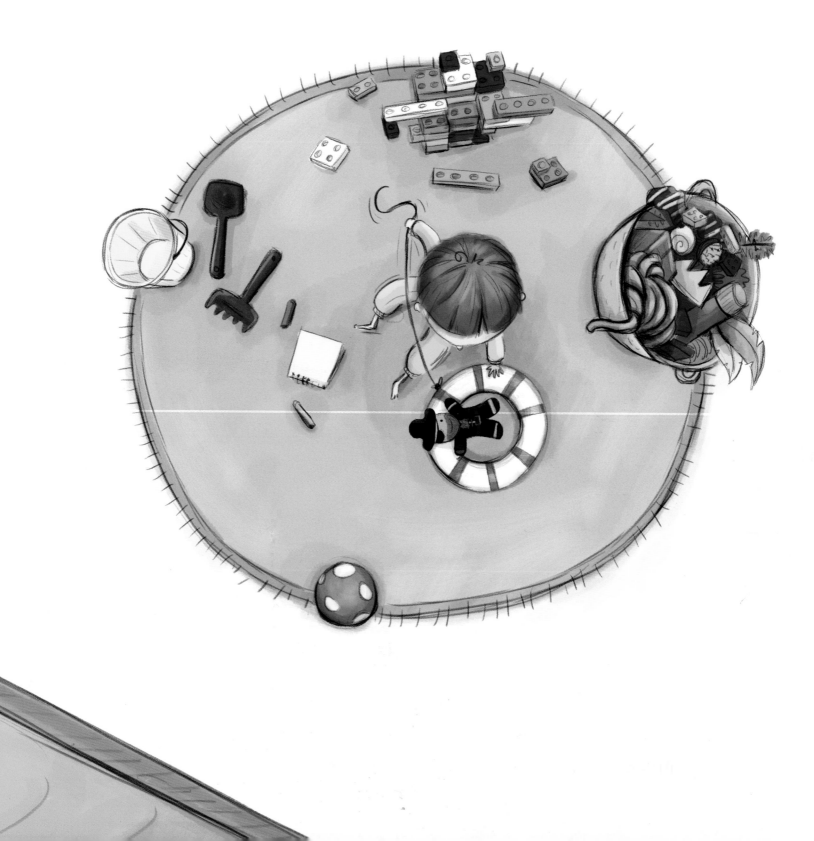

Then, something curious happened.

The book grew so swollen that it
rolled uncomfortably onto its side.

Soon, it could no longer be contained.

At first, there was a small trickle.
Just a drip ... drip ... drip.

In fact, if you listened closely,
you might think it was a dribbly
tap or a small leak in the roof.

'Dear, do you hear that?' asked J.J.'s mother.

'You're imagining things, Darling,' came the reply.

But a couple of stubborn imaginations would not stop the leak. The drip drips grew into plop plops. Puddles filled the living room.

Drip, drip! Drop, drop! Plop, plop! **Splish, splash!**

Surely it couldn't get any better!

A little ship sailed out of the book.

Mrs Blossburn picked up the ship and put it away with the other toys.

If you didn't know better, you might have mistaken the Blossburns' living room for an aquarium!

'Dear, I think I've just been nipped!' exclaimed J.J.'s mother.

'Don't be ridiculous, Darling.'

Before long, all manner
of creatures were making the
Blossburns' living room their own.

'Mind the octopus, Dear!'

'Hmm ... perhaps something is amiss after all.'

There was no stopping the book now!

But not all of the visitors were happy to find themselves swishing around an ordinary suburban home.

'Pirates, Darling!'

A great battle erupted between the Blossburns and the pirate intruders.

'Quick, pass the sword! Grab the cutlass! This is our living room, you swashbuckling rascals!'

Back and forth, back and forth. The swords clink-clinked and the water kept on coming.

Then a Kraken let out a terrifying roar! So loud was the roar that the Johnstons heard it three houses down.

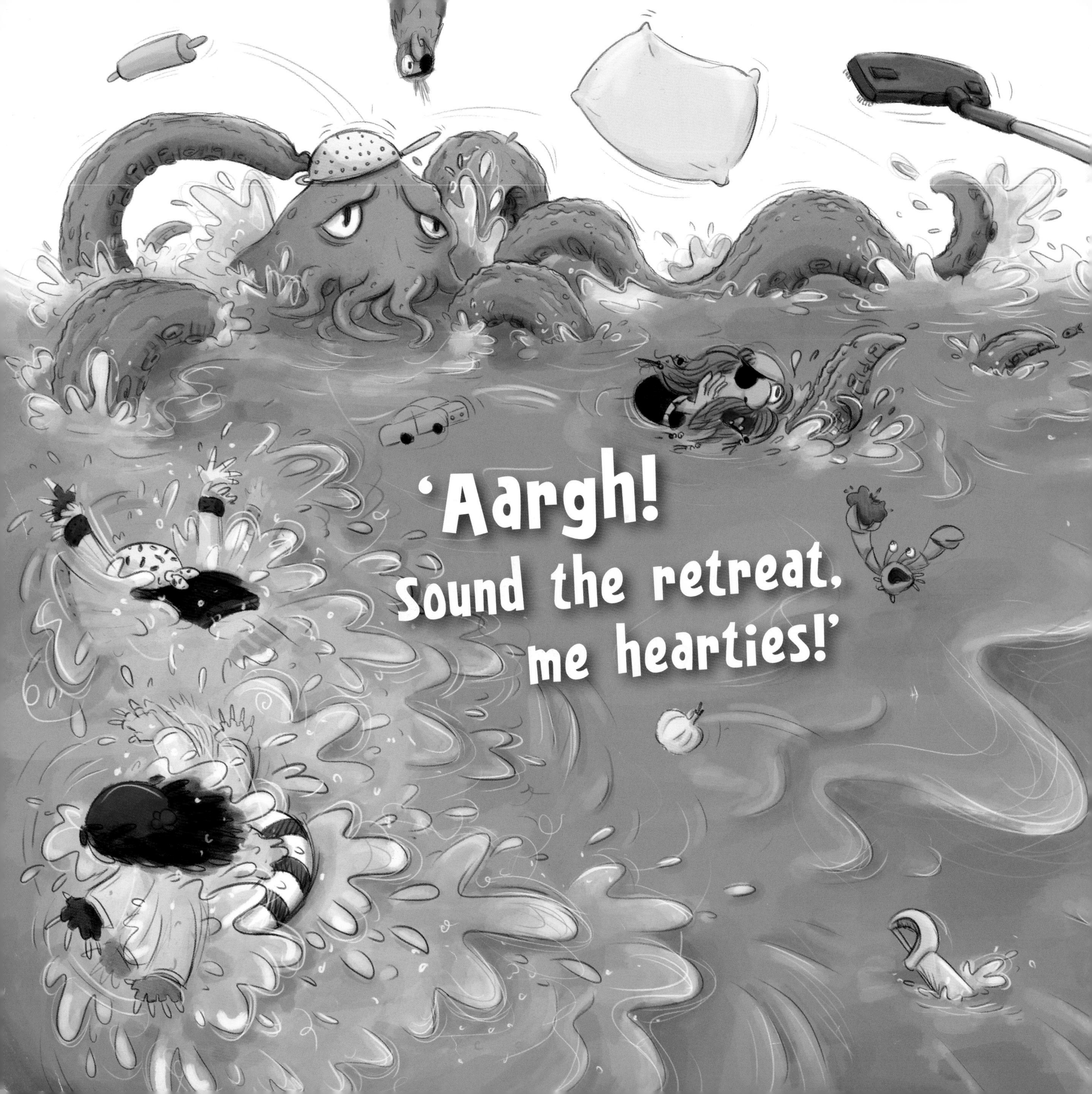

'Aargh!
Sound the retreat,
me hearties!'

The Blossburns grabbed anything they could use to fend off the uninvited guests.

Clearly, the pirates had underestimated their opponents.

'Find your own living room, this is ours!'

Then, as curiously as they had arrived, the awesome sea creatures began to shrink and the leak slowed.

The splishes and splashes turned
into plop plops then drop drops.

The drop drops turned into drip drips.

Finally, the book was sated.

'Phew! What an adventure!' said Dad.

'Perhaps we could go on another!'

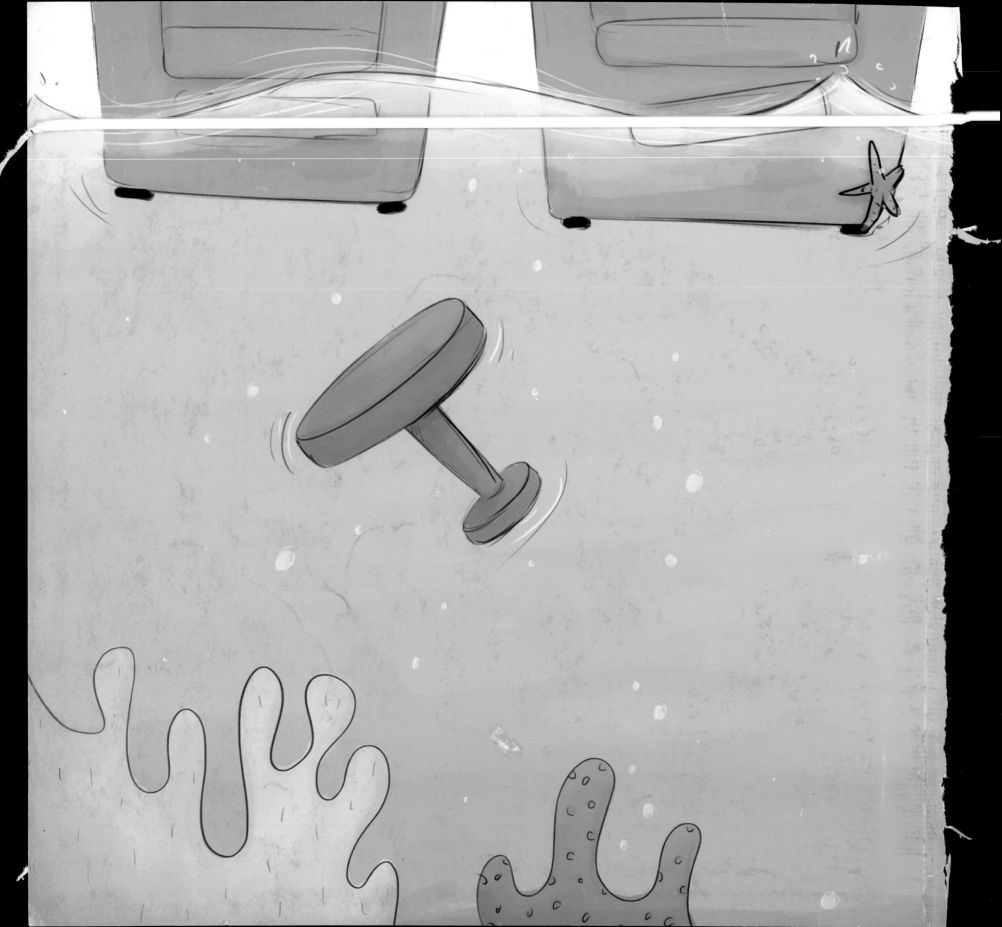